Teggs is no ordinary dinosaur –
he's an **ASTROSAUR!** Captain of
the amazing spaceship DSS *Sauropod*,
he goes on dangerous missions and
fights evil – along with his faithful
crew, Gipsy, Arx and Iggy.

For more astro-fun visit the website
www.astrosaurs.co.uk

Astrosaurs

THE HATCHING HORROR

Steve Cole

Illustrated by Charlie Fowkes

RED FOX

THE HATCHING HORROR
A RED FOX BOOK 978 1 849 41150 9

First published in Great Britain by Red Fox,
an imprint of Random House Children's Publishers UK
A Random House Group Company

First Red Fox edition published, 2005
This Red Fox edition published, 2010

9 10

Text copyright © Steve Cole, 2005
Illustrations copyright © Charlie Fowkes, 2005
Cover illustration and cards by Dynamo Design © Random House
Children's Books, 2010

The right of Steve Cole to be identified as the author of this work has been
asserted in accordance with the Copyright, Designs and Patents Act 1988.

Penguin Random House is committed to a sustainable future for
our business, our readers and our planet. This book is made from
Forest Stewardship Council® certified paper.

MIX
Paper from
responsible sources
FSC® C018179

Typeset in Bembo MT Schoolbook 16/20pt
by Falcon Oast Graphic Art Ltd.

Red Fox Books are published by Random House Children's Publishers UK,
61–63 Uxbridge Road, London W5 5SA

www.**randomhousechildrens**.co.uk
www.**randomhouse**.co.uk

Addresses for companies within The Random House Group Limited can be found
at: www.randomhouse.co.uk/offices.htm

THE RANDOM HOUSE GROUP Limited Reg. No. 954009

A CIP catalogue record for this book is available from the British Library.

Printed and bound in Great Britain by Clays Ltd, Elcograf S.p.A.

For Cassie and Nathan

WARNING!

THINK YOU KNOW ABOUT DINOSAURS?

THINK AGAIN!

The dinosaurs ...

Big, stupid, lumbering reptiles. Right?

All they did was eat, sleep and roar a bit. Right?

Died out millions of years ago when a big meteor struck the Earth. Right?

Wrong!

The dinosaurs weren't stupid. They may have had small brains, but they used them well. They had big thoughts and big dreams.

By the time the meteor hit, the last dinosaurs had already left Earth for ever. Some breeds had discovered how to travel through space as early as the Triassic period, and were already enjoying a new life among the stars. No one has found evidence of dinosaur technology yet. But the first fossil bones were only unearthed in 1822, and new finds are being made all the time.

The proof is out there, buried in the ground.

And the dinosaurs live on, way out in space, even now. They've settled down in a place they call the Jurassic Quadrant and over the last sixty-five million years they've gone on evolving.

 The dinosaurs we'll be meeting are part of a special group called the Dinosaur Space Service. Their job is to explore space, to go on exciting missions and to fight evil and protect the innocent!

These heroic herbivores are not just dinosaurs.

They are *astrosaurs*!

NOTE: The following story has been translated from secret Dinosaur Space Service records. Earthling dinosaur names are used throughout, although some changes have been made for easy reading. There's even a guide to help you pronounce the dinosaur names on the next page.

Talking Dinosaur!

How to say the prehistoric
names in this book . . .

STEGOSAURUS – *STEG-oh-SORE-us*

COMPSOGNATHUS – *komp-soh-NAY-thus*

PTEROSAUR – *TEH-roh-sore*

HADROSAUR – *HAD-roh-sore*

OVIRAPTOR – *OHV-ih-RAP-tor*

TRICERATOPS – *try-SERRA-tops*

DIMORPHODON – *die-MORF-oh-don*

IGUANODON – *ig-WA-noh-don*

ANKYLOSAURUS – *an-KI-loh-SORE-us*

THE CREW OF THE DSS SAUROPOD

**CAPTAIN
TEGGS STEGOSAUR**

ARX ORANO,
FIRST OFFICER

GIPSY SAURINE,
COMMUNICATIONS
OFFICER

IGGY TOOTH,
CHIEF ENGINEER

Jurassic Quadrant

Ankylos

Steggos

Diplox

INDEPENDEN
DINOSAUR
ALLIANCE

vegetarian sector

Squawk
Major

DSS
UNION OF
PLANETS

PTEROSAURIA

Tri System

Corytho

Lambeos

Iguanos

Aqua Minor

Geldos Cluster

Teerex
Major

Olympus

TYRANNOSAUR
TERRITORIES

Planet Sixty

carnivore
sector

Raptos

THEROPOD EMPIRE

Megalos

Cryptos

vegmeat
zone
(neutral space)

A REPTILE
SPACE

Pliosaur
Nurseries

Not to scale

THE
HATCHING
HORROR

Chapter One

THE EDGE OF EGG-STINCTION!

In a very big hall full of very big dinosaurs, a very big announcement was about to be made.

The Hall of Learning on the planet Odo Minor had never been more packed. Doctors, professors, scientists, TV cameras – they were all squashed up together. The sound of excited dinosaur chatter filled the hall. What was the big news? What had the great Professor Sog discovered now?

But two people in the hall already knew. And one of them didn't seem to care very much.

"I don't see why we had to come all this way!" grumbled Captain Teggs Stegosaur. "I haven't been in a learning hall since I passed my astrosaur exams!"

"Be patient, Captain," his companion Gipsy hissed. "As soon as the talk's over, our mission can begin!"

"About time too," Teggs declared. He was a captain in the Dinosaur Space Service, and he lived for adventure. With his brave crew of astrosaurs, he travelled through space in the DSS *Sauropod*, the finest ship in the Jurassic Quadrant.

Gipsy, a stripy hadrosaur, was his communications officer. She and Teggs had come here to escort Professor Sog back to the *Sauropod* – along with some very special guests . . .

She knew her crewmates would be busy up in orbit. Arx Orano, Teggs's brainy triceratops first officer, would be checking over the *Sauropod*'s systems. And Iggy Tooth, the tough iguanodon engineer, would be stoking the ship's mighty engines.

Their latest voyage into outer space would be their longest yet . . .

"At last," cheered Teggs, making Gipsy jump. "Here comes Professor Sog now!"

Sog was a small, twittery old creature who belonged to a breed called compsognathus. The audience hooted and stamped their feet politely as the funny little figure walked onto the stage. He stopped beside a mysterious, lumpy bundle hidden beneath a black blanket.

A great hush fell on the hall. The dinosaurs waited breathlessly for the professor's words.

Sog struggled to put on a small pair of spectacles. He had trouble reaching his head since his arms were so short. But finally he managed it, and he peered round at the curious crowd.

"Welcome, my friends," he cried. "You are about to hear of a most exciting discovery!"

A bright light started glowing above his head. Seconds later, a hologram of a large, long-necked dinosaur appeared. It looked a bit like a stegosaurus but with a longer neck and tail, and no spiky plates running down its back.

"This is a plateosaurus," said Sog. "Sweet, peaceful — and almost totally extinct."

"Extinct?" asked a puzzled journalist in the crowd.

Sog nodded sadly. "Their race has almost completely died out."

"Dined out?" asked Teggs, perking up. He was famous for his large appetite — some said it was the largest in the whole Dinosaur Space Service. "Dined out where? Can we come too?"

"Not dined out, *died* out!" groaned Gipsy.

Professor Sog continued his talk. "As you all know, we dinosaurs left the Earth long ago. We escaped in spaceships before the meteor struck, never to return. In those days there were many plateosaurus. Nowadays there are hardly any left."

"Why?" someone called.

"Homesickness," said Sog simply. "At

first, they settled on a fine planet called
Platus. But they didn't like it as much as
Earth, so they tried to return." He shook
his head sadly. "Their space fleet flew
into a cosmic storm. Many of their ships
were destroyed.
The few survivors
limped back to
Platus . . . to find
that T. rexes had
taken over."

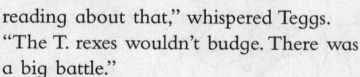

The audience
murmured their
disapproval.

"I remember
reading about that," whispered Teggs.
"The T. rexes wouldn't budge. There was
a big battle."

Gipsy nodded sadly. "And the
plateosaurus lost."

"Other vegetarian races came to
their aid," the professor went on. "As
you know, they joined together and

formed the Dinosaur Space Service, to protect all plant-eaters. In the end they kicked the T. rexes off Platus. But the little planet had been almost ruined by war."

The hologram switched off above Sog's head. "The plateosaurus race never recovered from the tragedy. Today, only a tiny handful survive." He shuffled closer to the black bundle beside him. "But now I bring new hope!"

He clamped his jaws down on the blanket and whipped it away. Beneath it was a pile of eight or nine large white eggs. The audience burst out in gasps and hoots. Flying reptiles flapped nearer with their

TV cameras to get a closer look.

"Plateosaurus eggs!" cried the little professor. "Discovered in a wrecked spaceship far out in the Jurassic Quadrant. That ship was a victim of the cosmic storm. It has drifted through space for thousands of years. But the eggs survived — frozen in space!"

The great hall filled with excited mutterings.

Professor Sog held up his feeble arms for quiet. "As you know, when it comes to hatching I am something of an expert . . ."

"*Eggs*-pert, more like!" Teggs chuckled.

"I was asked to study these old, old eggs," said Sog proudly. "And now that the eggs have thawed out, I believe that they will soon hatch! The plateosaurus race *will* live on!"

The audience cheered, and stamped their feet so hard that the floor shook.

"That's where we come in!" cried Teggs, rising to his feet. He flexed his long, bony tail, and knocked two elderly triceratops off their stools. "Oops!"

Sog frowned at the commotion. "Is that Captain Teggs?"

"Speaking!" he called cheerily, as Gipsy helped up the doddery dinosaurs. "Hello, everyone. It's my mission to take the professor, the eggs, and two plateosaurus guardians to a far-off world called Platus Two. A place where their race can make a fresh start!"

"*Is that a fact?!*"

Suddenly, the enormous wooden doors at the front of the hall were kicked open. The great hall rang with gasps of shock from the startled crowd.

Teggs narrowed his eyes. In the doorway stood a dozen small, ugly creatures. Their short, turtle-like heads bobbed about on scrawny necks.

One of the creatures darted towards the stage. "A fresh start for these lovely little hatchlings?" He shoved Professor Sog aside. "I don't think so! Not now the oviraptors are here!"

"Oviraptors?" frowned Teggs.

"Uh-oh!" Gipsy turned to Teggs in alarm. "They're nest-raiders! Egg-stealers!"

"We've got to stop them!" yelled Teggs. But he was blocked in on all sides by shocked old dinosaurs.

"I am Prince Goopo, and these are my royal brothers!" The oviraptor snatched up a plateosaurus egg and caressed it with his long, bony fingers. "Eggs are our favourite food, and eggs as rare as *these* will make a meal fit for a king – *and* his princes!" He threw back his head and laughed. "Forget your mission, Captain Teggs. The only place these eggs are going is *into our bellies*!"

Chapter Two

THE EGG-SNATCHERS

"Grub's up, lads!" yelled Prince Goopo.

The oviraptors raced into the learning hall. They moved like lightning. In a second they had stolen every last egg. Then they charged back out through the double doors.

"No!" yelled Teggs. "Get out of my way! They mustn't take the eggs!" He started pushing his way through the dinosaur audience. "You, near the front – stop them!"

But no one took any notice. They were rooted to the ground with shock at what they had just seen.

"Captain, wait!" called Gipsy.

"Catch me up, Gipsy!" Teggs had made it through the crowd, and now he was tearing down the gangway after the egg-snatchers. With a crash, he burst out of the learning hall and into the beautiful, snowy gardens. He shivered. Winter on Odo Minor was long and cold, and Teggs wished he'd worn his battle armour over his uniform to keep out the chill.

The learning hall was built on a high hilltop with a terrific view. One glance at the churned-up snow at his feet told Teggs where the speedy oviraptors had gone – straight down the hillside.

He charged off after them. Then a small oviraptor popped out from behind a tree – with a laser gun!

Zzzapp! A white-hot laser beam shot over Teggs's head.

"Thanks for warming me up!" Teggs called as he dived for the cover of a nearby bush.

"Just stay where you are, please!" said the oviraptor. He didn't sound as fierce as his brother on the stage. "I hate guns, and I'm a lousy shot."

Teggs frowned. "So why don't you just put down the gun and let me come out?"

"I'd love to," sighed the oviraptor. "But I can't. Goopo would throw a fit. He told me to stop anyone following us while he fetches the ship."

Teggs chewed some frozen leaves for extra strength. "Do you always do what your brother tells you?" he asked, creeping quietly closer.

"Goopo's the eldest. He'll be king someday." The little figure sighed. "I'm Prince Shelly, the youngest – so I never get any say in what goes on. Now, stay back! I don't want to hurt you!"

"That makes two of us!" called Teggs. Slowly, his big bony tail snaked out from the undergrowth and curled itself around Prince Shelly . . .

"Got you!" Teggs cried.

The oviraptor gasped as Teggs's tail tightened round him — he was trapped!

Teggs dragged his prisoner over to the top of the steep hillside. Goopo and his brothers were nearing the bottom of the slope. Soon they would vanish into the woods, and Teggs would never find them.

He dangled Shelly over the edge of the hillside. "You know, I think it's time you caught up with your brothers," he grinned. "There's *snow* time to lose!"

With that, Teggs flung Shelly down the hillside after his brothers. The raptor hit the snow with a yelp. Unable to stop himself, he rolled over and over. And as he rolled, he gathered snow — faster and faster. Soon, he looked like a giant squawking snowball. As he tumbled towards the fleeing oviraptors he got bigger and rounder and heavier . . .

Until finally – *Splat!* The snowball rolled right over Goopo and his brothers, squashing them into the snow.

"Direct hit!" cheered Teggs. Then he sledged down the hill on his tummy to round up the oviraptors and recover the eggs. Luckily, the soft snow had stopped them from breaking – and the oviraptors were unharmed too.

Up close, they were not pretty creatures. Their jaws were wide and toothless – instead, they used two bony prongs inside their mouths to crack open their food. Each of the creatures had a high, narrow crest rising up from its head.

Teggs smiled at the dazed reptiles. "That should cool you off till the space police arrive!"

"Curse you, Captain!" snarled Prince Goopo, half-buried by snow. "I command you to release us in the name of our king!"

"No way," said Teggs. "Anyway, I'm
sure your king would be very cross if
he knew you were stealing such
important eggs!"

"Pah!" cried Goopo. "It
was his idea! King Albu
will kill us if we don't
bring him those eggs!"

"He'll fry us with butter!"
twittered another oviraptor.

"He'll boil us in salty water for three
minutes!" moaned a third.

"And then he'll crack our heads with
a big spoon!" quaked one more.

"It's quite exhausting," sighed
Prince Shelly, still stuck
in his giant snowball.
"Me and my brothers
are sent out round the
universe in search of
tasty new treats for
the royal menu. Goopo's
right. If we fail . . .

the king will have us served with toast soldiers!"

Just then, Gipsy came scampering down the hill. "There you are, Captain!" she beamed as she reached the bottom. "I see you've caught the thieves!"

Teggs winked at her. "Better still, the eggs are safe and sound!"

Gipsy frowned. "But, Captain—"

Whatever Gipsy said, Teggs didn't hear it. For with a mighty roar of engines, a strange spaceship rose up into the sky above the forest. It was a long, narrow rocket with two spinning engines at one end, like an enormous egg-whisk.

Goopo laughed. "Using Shelly to squash us was a good trick, Captain," he said. "But Prince Hibbit was too quick for you! He got away to the woods and fetched the ship!"

Teggs and Gipsy backed away as the spaceship came in to land. Prince Hibbit was leaning out of the window, pulling rude faces. The heat from the ship's whisking engines soon melted the nearby snow, and his brothers shook themselves free.

Hibbit fired a laser bolt at Teggs. It missed by millimetres. He and Gipsy were forced back.

"Get on board, brothers!" Goopo cried. "We won't be cracked, scrambled, and mixed with mayonnaise *this* day!"

In the wink of an eye, the soggy oviraptors had bundled back on board with the stolen eggs. Shelly was the last inside. With a sad little wave at Teggs and Gipsy, he vanished into the ship. It took off at once.

Teggs spoke into the communicator strapped to his arm. "Teggs to *Sauropod*! Arx, can you hear me? An oviraptor ship is getting away! Stop them!" He looked helplessly at Gipsy. "I don't believe it! I've let them take the eggs — I've failed!"

Chapter Three

EXPECT THE UN-EGGS-PECTED!

On the flight deck of the DSS *Sauropod*, high above the planet, Arx Orano heard his captain's cry.

"Quick!" the triceratops barked at his flight crew. "Switch on the scanners! Find that spaceship!"

The flight crew were dimorphodon, highly trained flying reptiles. They clucked and flapped about the dinosaur

spaceship, pulling levers and flicking switches.

The scanner soon showed the oviraptor ship soaring away at top speed.

"Fire lasers!" Arx ordered.

Beams of light fired from the *Sauropod*. But the oviraptor ship quickly whisked away out of range. Not a single shot found its mark.

Arx sighed and nudged the communicator with his nose horn. "Captain? This is Arx. I'm afraid the oviraptors were too quick for us. They've got away!"

★

Captain Teggs felt awful as he walked back to the Hall of Learning. His head hung down in shame. Gipsy patted him on the side of his neck with a gentle hoof. "It's all right, Captain," she said. "There's nothing to worry about!"

"Oh yeah?" Teggs waved his spiky tail towards the crowds that were starting to spill out from the hall. "Let's see if *they* agree with you!"

Professor Sog was leading his fellow dinosaurs outside. The perky little reptile was hopping about with excitement.

"Well done,
Captain!" he
chirped. "Your
concern was very
convincing. Those
oviraptors are bound
to think they've stolen
the *real* eggs!"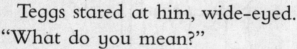

Teggs stared at him, wide-eyed.
"What do you mean?"

"Those eggs on the stage were fakes!"
Sog chuckled. "They were just props! I
brought them along to spice up my
talk."

Teggs whooped with relief. "Then
where *are* the real eggs?"

"Here!" came a low, lazy voice from
the crowd. Two large, long-necked
creatures stomped into view. Teggs
recognized them from the professor's
hologram — they were plateosaurus.
They each carried a large shiny box
around their necks.

"I am Coo," said one of the dinosaurs.

"And I am Dippa," said the other, a female. "We are the guardians of the eggs."

Coo bobbed his head at the box round Dippa's neck. "I watch her eggs."

"And I watch his," Dippa explained.

"So now the mission can begin!" Professor Sog was still merrily leaping about. "Oh, I'd love to see King Albu's face when he tries to eat those eggs!"

Way out in space, at the sticky centre of his royal ship, King Albu sat waiting on his golden throne. Thick drool bubbled out of his mouth and stained his royal robes at the thought of his next meal — fried plateosaurus eggs on toast!

King Albu waited.

And waited.

His tummy rumbled loud enough to make the walls shake. And *still* he waited.

At last, King Albu could bear it no more. He turned to the nearest slave and shouted: "Fetch me Prince Goopo — now!"

The slave rushed from the room. Less than a minute later, Prince Goopo came in. He looked very worried.

"Where are my eggs?" hissed King Albu.

Prince Goopo gulped. "I think . . . er . . . I think Cook was having a little trouble bringing out their full flavour . . ."

"Fetch me the cook at once!" screamed King Albu.

Prince Goopo crawled out of the room at top speed. In seconds, he had returned with the cook, who looked red-faced and nervous.

"Where's my supper?" roared the king.

"Erm . . ." The cook crossed his legs like he needed the toilet. "They are . . . er . . . very tough to cook."

"So?" growled King Albu. "Just serve 'em up as they are!"

"Forgive me, Your

Egginess," said the cook. "But I really don't think—"

"Look, Cook. I like 'em soft. I like 'em hard. I like sucking out the yolk with a straw. I like paddling in the egg whites then licking my feet clean."

The slaves nodded solemnly. They had seen him do such things lots of times.

"I like 'em raw. I like 'em fried. I like 'em thin. I like 'em wide." King Albu narrowed his eyes and widened his mouth. "In short, *I like my eggs*, Cook! And I want a piled-up plate of plateosaurus eggs right now!"

The cook sighed and went outside. He returned with a silver trolley piled high with a grassy salad — and several giant eggs.

"At last!" drooled the king. He grasped an egg in both hands. Then he opened his mouth as wide as it would go, and popped it inside.

Where it stuck!

The egg could not be crushed or chewed or slurped down or guzzled. It stuck right in his throat. King Albu's scaly neck looked like a snake that had swallowed a rugby ball!

"Urph!" he choked. "That's not an egg! It's a *rock*! A painted rock!" He ran around, clutching the large lump in his neck. "You idiot, Goopo! I send you out for eggs and you bring back *boulders*!"

With a strangled yell, King Albu choked up the enormous fake egg and kicked it across the room.

"My stomach wants plateosaurus eggs!" he panted. "And my stomach will not take no for an answer! Get your brothers together, Goopo. We're going to get our hands on those eggs — whatever it takes!"

Chapter Four

THE LONG, LONG JOURNEY

Back on Odo Minor, Iggy the engineer was waiting for his captain in the *Sauropod*'s shuttle. When Teggs poked his head through the door, the iguanodon saluted stiffly.

"Ready for boarding, Captain!" he cried.

"It's going to be a tight squeeze, Iggy!" grinned Teggs. He came aboard, with Gipsy close behind. Then Coo and Dippa squeezed in through the shuttle's doorway. They shuffled close together and Professor Sog hopped aboard beside them.

"I still can't believe the oviraptors went to all that trouble just to steal a lot of painted rocks!" laughed Teggs. "That'll give King Albu an upset tummy!"

"It sure will," laughed Gipsy, as the shuttle blasted off into space. "And meanwhile, we'll make sure the *real* eggs reach Platus Two – safe and sound and ready for hatching!"

Soon the *Sauropod* was racing through space.

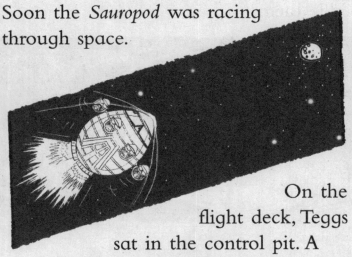

On the flight deck, Teggs sat in the control pit. A feeling of excitement was building in his belly. His mission had begun. And with the eggs almost ready to hatch, there was no time to lose!

Arx turned on the scanner. Tiny stars gleamed in the darkness of space. "That's where we're headed," he said.

"The very edge of the galaxy."

Professor Sog nodded his little head. "I'm looking forward to seeing Platus Two!"

Gipsy wrinkled her snout, puzzled. "You mean you haven't been there before?"

"No one's been there for hundreds of years," Sog told her. "Not since it was first discovered by the Jurassic Explorers."

"Wow," breathed Teggs. The Jurassic Explorers were his heroes. They were the reason he had become an astrosaur. Long before he was born, they had discovered and mapped the entire

Jurassic Quadrant, where all dinosaurs now lived. The only thing they had never found was a star dragon — a huge, winged animal that was said to live somewhere in space. It was Teggs's dream that maybe one day he would find a star dragon himself.

"Why has no one ever gone to live on Platus Two?" asked Gipsy.

"It's too small and far away from everywhere else," said Sog.

"So we'll be the first spaceship to go there in centuries!" Teggs realized.

Arx nodded. "I wonder what it's like?"

"It'll be lovely, just you wait and see!" smiled Sog. "The explorers planted lots of seeds there. After hundreds of years it should be

40

very green indeed!" He chuckled. "Yes, Platus Two may be too far away to matter to most dinosaurs. But it's the perfect spot for a small herd of peaceful plateosaurus!"

"Hope so," sighed Coo. "A new home would be nice, wouldn't it, Dippa?"

"It would, Coo," Dippa agreed.

Just then the ship shook with a sudden *clunk!* The dimorphodon flight crew squawked and then flapped in panic about the room.

"Battle stations!" cried Teggs.

Arx squinted at his instruments. "No sign of hostile ships," he reported. "Only a meteor, bouncing off the side of the ship."

"Oh," said Teggs, a tiny bit disappointed.

"Funny," said Arx. "It seems to be following us."

"It must have got caught in our gravity field," said Professor Sog.

"I suppose so," Arx nodded. "But I've never known a meteor do that before."

"We're out in deep space now," said Gipsy. She looked a bit spooked. "Who knows what we'll find out here?"

"We'll find Platus Two, that's what!" said Sog firmly. "Don't let your imagination run away with you, child!"

But as the *Sauropod* sped on to its destination, Gipsy found it was hard not to.

Days passed by and the stars grew fewer and fainter.

Space grew blacker and blacker.

And Captain Teggs began to grow bored. For the first few days he'd kept a careful watch for star dragons. But he could find no sign of one anywhere.

By the end of the first week, the scanner was showing nothing but blackness. The *Sauropod* was like a big fish swimming through the darkest sea in the universe.

"Hey, that's strange," said Arx, looking at a computer screen. "We're *still* dragging along that meteor we bumped into."

"Never mind boring old meteors," said Teggs. "Who's for another game of I-Spy?"

The days dragged on. But at the end of the *second* week, they could at last see Platus Two on the scanners.

And Arx made a strange discovery.

He called everyone to the flight deck to tell them about it.

"Well, Arx?" said Teggs, settling back into the control pit after a long doze.

"I've been studying Platus Two closely, Captain," the triceratops announced. "And something's wrong. I've checked my findings against the notes made by the Jurassic Explorers – and they're completely different!"

Teggs frowned as he chewed some moss. "Different in what way?"

Arx looked at him. "Since the Jurassic Explorers visited Platus Two, it has grown *ten times bigger*!"

"Impossible!" Sog said crossly. He tried to fold his arms but they wouldn't quite reach, which made him even crosser. "Planets do not grow like living things! Arx, you must be wrong! Your instruments are faulty!"

At that, Arx got a bit huffy, and Teggs quickly butted in before a big row started.

"Can you show us Platus Two on the scanners, Arx?" he asked.

Arx jabbed a button with his horn. On the screen, Platus Two glowed bright against black space. Pure white and smooth, it looked like a giant snooker ball.

Then a rocky shape drifted into view.

"It's that stupid meteor again," grumbled Arx.

"But I thought it was trailing behind us," said Teggs. "How come it's now heading *straight for us*?"

A split-second later, Teggs got his answer. Everyone jumped as the meteor suddenly split right open! Bursting from inside it — like a terrifying creature hatching from a giant egg — was a familiar whisk-like ship.

"Oviraptors!" gasped Gipsy.

Arx nodded grimly. "They disguised their ship as a meteor and tagged along all the way here!"

"They want our eggs!" wailed Coo.

"Oh dear," said Dippa.

Suddenly the oviraptor ship fired its lasers. Two balls of flame streaked towards them.

"Red alert!" shouted Teggs. "We're under attack!"

Chapter Five

LIGHTNING STRIKES TWICE

Twin bolts of fire slammed into the
Sauropod. The ship shook like a jelly in
an earthquake. Then it tipped up. Coo
and Dippa screamed, their egg boxes
clanging together like giant bells.
Professor Sog was sent somersaulting
up to the ceiling. The dimorphodon
flight crew screeched and flapped into
each other.

Teggs fought to keep his balance in the control pit. Flapping reptiles collided above him. The squawk of the alarm pterosaur echoed round the ship: "*Red alert! Red alert!*"

"Damage report!" cried Teggs.

Iggy came tumbling out of the lift and onto the flight deck. "Message from the engine room, Captain!" he yelled. "Engines have been hit!"

"We can't get away now!" cried Sog, as a pair of flying reptiles helped him down from the ceiling.

"Fire lasers," snapped Teggs.

"Lasers have jammed!" Gipsy reported.

"All right then, fire the dung torpedoes!" he ordered.

Gipsy flicked a row of switches with her tail. "Firing now!"

On the scanner, a brown explosion lit up the oviraptor ship. "Direct hit!" cheered Arx.

"That should cause a stink on the oviraptor ship!" grinned Iggy.

"Message coming in," Gipsy reported. "It's King Albu!"

"Put him on screen," Teggs said.

Everyone watched as an ugly, stubby little creature appeared on the screen. He wore a large crown on his head and an even larger clothes peg on his snout.

Teggs smiled grimly. "I see that you've felt — and smelled — what our dung torpedoes can do, King Albu. Leave now, and we'll say no more about it."

King Albu shook his head. "Doo hab dum-fing I vant, Dap-tin," he hissed.

"Er . . . pardon?" asked Teggs.

The royal oviraptor pulled the peg from his nose. "I said, you have something I want, Captain!"

"You really came all this way just to eat the plateosaurus eggs?" Teggs shook his head sadly. "You have to be crazy!"

"I certainly am," King Albu agreed. "So hand them over — or else my power poachers will turn you into toast!"

Teggs shook his head. "Try that and the next round of dung torpedoes will knock your noses clean off!"

"I don't think so, Captain." King Albu smiled nastily. "Your engines run on dung, and we've just blasted them open. You can't afford to waste any more fuel."

Iggy sighed. "He's right, Captain!"

"Oh well," sighed Coo. "I suppose we'd better let him have the eggs, then."

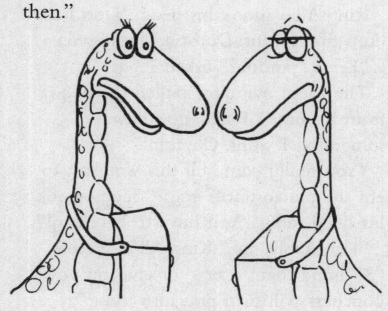

"Yes, that's probably best," agreed Dippa. "Never mind."

"Never mind?" Teggs stared at them. "This is the future of your people we're talking about!"

"But there's nothing we can do," said Coo.

"There's always *something* we can do," said Teggs bravely.

"Like what?" asked Professor Sog.

Everyone looked at Teggs.

"Well . . . we need to repair our engines. And for that, we need to land." He nodded firmly. "We must head for Platus Two. Now!"

"But we can't outrun King Albu, Captain!" said Iggy.

"We have to try!" Teggs snapped.

"We might just lose them in the clouds. Maybe we'll buy enough time to fix the damage."

"It's a brave plan, Captain," said Arx with a small smile.

Gipsy clapped her claws together and called to the flight crew. "Let's do it, team!"

The *Sauropod*'s engines hummed weakly. With a lurch, they were off.

"Don't say I didn't warn you, Captain!" snarled King Albu. He put the clothes peg back on his nose and turned to his crew. "Dopen vire!" he shouted.

"Eh?" Teggs frowned.

An ear-splitting explosion ripped through the *Sauropod*. The whole ship shook even harder than before.

"He said, 'Open fire'," said Arx helpfully.

"Approaching Platus Two," said Gipsy. "Entering clouds now."

"Take that oviraptor off the screen!"
said Teggs. "Let's have a look!"

King Albu's evil face was replaced by
a close-up view of the cloudy white
planet.

"Take us in low," Teggs ordered.
"We'll try to steer round behind him
and stay out of sight."

"Such a shame," sighed Sog. "We're
already fighting over this calm and
peaceful world."

"Er . . . calm and peaceful, you say?"

echoed Teggs, looking at the screen.

They had broken through the clouds. Now they could see what the planet was really like.

It was horrible.

The pale ground was smooth and speckled, but criss-crossed with huge cracks as if it was ready to fall apart. There were no hills or trees, no flowers or animals. Everywhere was flat and featureless, and a fierce storm was raging overhead. Lightning hurled bright daggers down at the ground. Great fountains of sticky lava spurted up to the clouds in revenge.

Dippa sighed. "Not very green, is it?"

"But — but this is terrible!" squawked Professor Sog. "The explorers planted seeds! Why haven't they grown?"

"*Now* will you believe me?" said Arx. "This can't be Platus Two at all. It's a different world!"

"No!" Sog insisted. "I checked the

star charts! This is right where Platus Two should be!"

Coo and Dippa just stared sadly at the screen.

"Captain!" shouted Gipsy. "The oviraptors have found us! Look!"

King Albu's ship was swooping out of the clouds towards them.

"We have to go faster!" Teggs cried.

"We can't!" yelled Iggy.

Then, just as everything seemed hopeless, a jagged blast of yellow light struck the oviraptor ship – and it fell from the sky like a stone.

"Lightning!" beamed Teggs. "King Albu's ship has been struck by lightning!"

"Serves them right," said Iggy.

"We're saved!" Professor Sog did a little victory jig. "Yippee!"

But suddenly, the scanner glowed white-hot. A crisp crackling noise rasped through the air. Sparks flew round the flight deck. Sog stopped dancing, and the dimorphodon flapped round in panic.

"Ooops," said Arx. "Now *we've* been struck by lightning!"

The engines spluttered and died.

"We're going down!" shouted Iggy.

"Attention, crew!" Teggs yelled. "Brace yourselves! We're going to crash!"

"We're going to crash!" squawked the alarm pterosaur. "*We're going to crash!*"

On the scanner, the ground came rushing up to meet them . . .

Chapter Six

THE MYSTERIOUS PLANET

Ka-boom!

Tumbling out of control, the *Sauropod* scraped against the smooth surface of the planet.

B-B-B-B-B-B-B-B-Bang!

The ship flipped up and over. It splattered through one of the red-hot geysers spurting out of the ground.

"She can't take much more!" howled Iggy.

"Neither can we!" gasped Dippa.

A long, wide crack had opened up beneath them. The *Sauropod* fell through the crack and started bouncing between the sides. Then a fresh spurt of sticky lava pushed them high up into the air.

Teggs braced himself. "What goes up, must come down!"

At last, the final crash came.

No one on board the *Sauropod* had ever heard a noise like it.

It was a crumpling, rumpling, bone-crushing, head-mushing, grinding, gruelling, wrenching, bottom-clenching *smash*.

Then the ship was still.

Slowly, Coo raised his long, aching neck. "I wish I'd stayed at home," he sighed.

"Now we know how the meteor felt when it smashed into the Earth," groaned Teggs.

Professor Sog peered out from under a chair. "The eggs!" he twittered. "Dippa, Coo – what about the eggs?"

The two plateosaurus checked their egg boxes.

"Unscrambled," Dippa reported.

"Wish I could say the same for my brains," said Teggs.

Iggy waddled over to the communicator. "Calling engine room, this is Iggy. Are you all right, boys?"

Assorted moans and groans came from the speaker.

"Just about!" someone said.

"Good," said Teggs. "Everyone's OK. But remember, if *we* made it through the landing, chances are that King Albu and his egg-snatchers did too." He hungrily uprooted an enormous fern and swallowed it down. "And there's nothing like a really big crash for working up an appetite!"

"Perhaps we should *all* get eating," said Arx gravely. "We need to make more fuel for the engines."

"Of course," said Gipsy, wrinkling her nose. "More dung!"

"It's a big job," said Teggs. "*Several* big jobs, in fact."

"Leave it to me and my boys," smiled Iggy. "We'll have a good meal while we fix the engines. Then we'll fill them up for you — no sweat!"

Teggs saluted him. "I knew I could count on you!"

Iggy saluted in return, and left the flight deck.

Gipsy pulled a face. "Well, while Iggy gets to the *bottom* of things in the engine room, I'll try to listen in on the oviraptors."

"Good idea," said Teggs. "We might learn what they're planning."

Gipsy's hands flicked over the controls. Suddenly, a spooky wailing sound crackled out of the speakers.

"What is *that*?" asked Teggs.

"Sounds like a ghost!" said Dippa.

"Or faulty speakers," Arx added.

"I think it sounded like someone in distress," said Gipsy. She pressed some more buttons. "Yes, I've got a fix on the signal now. It's coming from somewhere outside!"

"Impossible!" snapped Professor Sog. "How could anyone live in this terrible place?"

"We'd better find out," said Teggs. "Because if we can't get the ship fixed – we'll be joining them!"

The crew got ready to go outside. Then they gathered at the ship's main hatchway.

Teggs had changed into his battle armour, and Gipsy had slipped on her combat suit. If it came to a fight, they would be ready.

Gipsy joined Teggs as he stared out onto the strange, dark planet.

"Do you think we'll really get out of this mess?" she whispered.

"We've got to, Gipsy," said Teggs softly. He gave her a crooked smile. "I can't stop exploring space yet! I haven't discovered my very own star dragon!"

"Speaking of discoveries . . ." said Arx, shuffling over. "I wonder what we'll find out there?"

"Well, whoever was making that noise, we can find them with this," said Gipsy, tapping a gadget on her wrist. "It's a special tracker. The faster it bleeps, the closer we are."

"Why can't we just hide on the *Sauropod* until Iggy's fixed the engines?" asked Dippa.

Teggs shook his head. "If the oviraptors come aboard, they'll sniff out the eggs in seconds. Out there in the storm, they'll find it harder. Besides, Iggy and the boys have some important jobs to do. They mustn't be put off by a load of rotten reptiles running about."

Just then, a flash of lightning lit up

the sky. Gipsy thought she caught a glimpse of something moving just outside.

"We'd better get going," she said nervously.

Teggs led the way out onto the surface of the unpleasant planet, through the howling wind and the drenching rain. The ground was smooth and slippery beneath their feet. He had the feeling they were being watched.

Lightning flashed again. Teggs caught a sudden movement from the corner of his eye. Dark shapes, small and nasty, creeping towards them.

"Look out!" he yelled. "It's the oviraptors!"

"It sure is," gurgled Goopo.

"Worst luck for you!" snarled King Albu.

He snapped his claws

and his sons rushed to form a tight
circle around the dinosaurs. Teggs saw
now that each of them held a ray gun.

"We're trapped!" gasped Gipsy.

Arx lowered his horns. "I could
charge them, Captain."

"They'd blast you before you got
close," hissed Teggs. "I won't let them
add roast triceratops to their mad
menu!"

"Now then, Captain Teggs," said King Albu. "You know what I want: eggs!" A dreamy look came into his eyes. "Yes, I said eggs! E-G-G-S. Eggs, eggs, eggs, eggs." He started drooling. "Eggggggggggggggs, mmmmmm."

One by one, his sons started dribbling too. "Egggggggs," they echoed.

But not Prince Shelly. He threw down his gun crossly. "This is *silly*, Father!" he complained. "Our ship's lying in pieces! We're stranded billions of miles from home! And all you care about are a few lousy eggs!"

"Lousy?" gasped King Albu in shock. "You dare . . . to call eggs . . . *lousy*?"

The oviraptors all booed and hissed Prince Shelly.

And while they were distracted, Teggs struck.

He lashed out with his armoured tail. Blue sparks shot from the end, and four of the little reptiles were sent flying.

"Now, Arx!" Teggs cried.

The triceratops charged at Prince Goopo, who cried out in terror and ran. He screeched so loudly that the others dropped their guns as they scrabbled to block their ears.

Then Gipsy sprang into action. With

a few well-placed jabs, kicks and tail-swipes she flattened five more of the oviraptors.

But King Albu had grabbed one of the ray guns. He started firing wildly. Bolts of white light sizzled through the air.

"Run!" cried Teggs as one of the laser beams whistled past his ear.

Rushing for cover, Arx and Coo went one way while Gipsy and Sog went another. Dippa ran off all by herself, so

Teggs chased after her.

"Just you wait, acorn-brain!" roared King Albu. "I'll get those eggs yet!"

"Not if I can help it," muttered Teggs. He swung his head about wildly, looking for somewhere to hide from the gunfire. But the landscape was smooth and flat on all sides.

"Look out!" called Dippa.

Teggs skidded to a stop just in front of a huge gash in the ground. It was too wide to jump over.

"We'll have to turn back!" wailed Dippa.

"We can't!" said Teggs. As if to prove it, a laser beam whizzed past between them. "There's only one place we can go now!"

Teggs was pointing to the crack in the ground. "Down *there*?" Dippa gulped.

"Now!" cried Teggs.

Together, the two dinosaurs leaped into the blackness.

Chapter Seven

THE TUNNELS OF FEAR

Luckily, Teggs and Dippa didn't have far to fall. They landed with a thump on a small ledge.

"Did you know this was here?" gasped Dippa.

"Er . . . of course!" said Teggs quickly.

Dippa peered over the edge. "How deep is this crack?" she wondered. "And what's at the bottom of it?"

A spooky, wailing noise rose up from the darkness. It was the same noise they had heard back on the *Sauropod*.

"Who needs Gipsy's tracker?" said Teggs. "Whatever that thing is, it's right beneath us!" He explored along the ledge a little further. Soon the winking lights on his battle helmet lit up a jagged gash in the smooth rock beside him. "It's another crack . . . a sort of passageway! Come on, before the oviraptors find us."

"I don't like scary passageways," whispered Dippa. "Why don't we just let King Albu *have* the eggs?"

Teggs stared at her. "How can you even think such a thing?"

Dippa shrugged. "It would be much easier."

"It would be easier, but it would be *wrong*," said Teggs sternly. "Those eggs hold the future of your race! Isn't that worth fighting for?"

"Fighting ruined our old world," said Dippa. "Fighting is bad."

"But giving up is bad too, Dippa," Teggs told her. "I know you're scared. I am too! But you mustn't throw away your dreams."

Dippa nodded slowly. "I dream of a new place to call home," she said. "I dream of having little baby plateosaurus to look after. I dream that one day there will be a whole, happy herd of us on our own planet."

"Then *fight* for those dreams," Teggs told her.

Just then, they heard a scuttling sound above them. "This way, boys!" came a familiar, wicked voice. "There's a ledge! They must have jumped down here!"

"King Albu!" hissed Teggs. "Quick!
Let's get going!"

He and Dippa started galloping
through the darkness on all fours. The
oviraptors soon figured out where they
had gone, and gave chase.

"They're catching up!" panted Dippa.

"Keep running!" cried Teggs.

Then the mysterious, ghostly wail
started up again, chilling them to the
bone. Teggs and Dippa skidded to a
halt, and so did the oviraptor princes.
Teggs saw them by the light of his

battle helmet, clutching each other in fear.

"We — we *have* to go back now, Father!" stammered Shelly.

"Never!" cried King Albu. "Now, grab those eggs, boys — or I'll hard-boil you all!"

Goopo and his brothers slowly advanced on the two herbivores.

"Get behind me, Dippa," hissed Teggs. "Maybe I can scare them off." He flexed his armoured tail, ready to fight. But the passage was too small, and his tail was too big. It whacked against the smooth wall and suddenly, the whole passageway started to shake.

"Look out, Dippa!" shouted Teggs. "The walls are caving in!"

"Eeek!" squeaked Goopo. He turned and fled, his brothers close behind. Teggs and Dippa huddled together as big speckled slabs kept on falling. Soon the passage was completely blocked. They were safe from the oviraptors – but now there was no way back to the *Sauropod*.

"There's only one path we can take now," said Teggs quietly. "But it'll lead us right to whatever's been making that terrible noise!"

Meanwhile, Gipsy and Sog were huddled outside in a howling gale, wishing they were warm and safe back on the *Sauropod*. Like Teggs and Dippa, they had hidden in one of the great splits in the planet's surface. But the ledge they were creeping along was very narrow. One slip, and they would fall to their doom.

"I wonder what caused all these cracks," said Sog nervously. "If it was an earthquake, where's all the rubble? There's not a single loose stone round here!"

"Maybe it's special, super-tough rock," said Gipsy. "That's why the explorers' seeds never grew." Gipsy's tracker started beeping loudly. "You know, this thing is going crazy. It reckons the source of that signal is . . . everywhere!"

"Shhh!" gasped the little professor. "I think something's coming!"

He was right. Something heavy was creeping along the ledge in the opposite direction — straight towards them.

"It's too dark!" hissed Gipsy. "I can't see what it is!"

"It's the thing that made that terrible wailing noise!" cried Sog. "I know it is!"

He hopped onto Gipsy's tail and
scampered up to her shoulder in fright.
  The footsteps shuffled closer and
closer . . .

Chapter Eight

THE SECRET OF PLATUS TWO

"Halt!" squawked Professor Sog
bravely. He peered out from behind the
crest on Gipsy's head. "Who goes
there?"

A familiar figure came out of the
shadows. "Hello, Gipsy! Professor!"

"Arx!" squealed Gipsy in delight.

"And me!" called Coo from somewhere behind him.

"Thank goodness!" gasped Sog. "So, you hid in the crack too!"

"There was nowhere else to go," said Arx. He seemed a little out of breath. "I'm glad we've found you. There's something I think you should see."

"What is it?" asked Gipsy.

But Arx was already retracing his footsteps. "The path gets very steep down here. Don't slip!"

Gipsy and Sog followed them along the ledge. Arx was right – the path dipped down sharply. Gipsy trod carefully, while Sog slithered down on his bottom.

The air grew warmer. The ledge grew wider. A soft, thudding noise seemed to echo up from the chasm beside them.

To Gipsy, it sounded like a huge,

heavy heartbeat. Her tracker bleeped so loudly she had to turn it off.

They crept on for what felt like ages. Then, suddenly, the steep path levelled out. Arx came to a sudden stop.

"Here we are," he said. "A hole. I think it stretches down to the very centre of the planet!"

Gipsy stared down into the hole. This was the source of the heartbeat sound: *Ba-DUMP . . . Ba-DUMP . . . Ba-DUMP . . .*

It was like looking into a deep well. Far below, thick yellowy–white liquid sloshed about like runny custard.

"Keep watching," Arx murmured.

Then, just below the slimy surface of the goo . . . something massive moved!

"What was that?" Gipsy gasped.

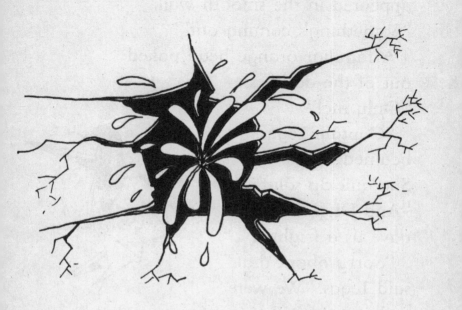

"I think I know," said Arx. "But if I'm right, we're in worse trouble than we thought!"

Even as he spoke, the wall behind them exploded with a mighty crash!

Coo yelped as bits of the strange, smooth rock flew through the air. Sog hid behind Arx's head for safety.

Gipsy whirled around in surprise. "Look!" she cried. A huge hole had

appeared in the smooth wall.
"Something's coming out!"

A familiar orange head poked
out of the darkness.
"Only me!"

"Captain Teggs!"
beamed Gipsy.
She quickly saluted.
"And Dippa! You
gave us a fright!"

"Sorry about that,"
said Teggs. "We were
walking through one of the cracks,
but it came to a dead end."

"So he smashed through the rock
with his tail!" added Dippa.

"Rock, eh?" said Arx. He nudged a
fragment of the smooth rock with his
horn. "I'm not so sure . . . See how
easily this stuff breaks?"

Teggs looked hurt. "Well, I did give it
quite a whack, you know!"

"I'm sure you did, Captain," said Arx

quickly. "But look at it! So smooth, so brittle. It's not really like rock at all, is it?"

Everyone stared at the broken pieces on the ground.

"You're right," said Teggs slowly. "In fact, it looks a lot like . . . *eggshell*!"

"Eggshell?" twittered Sog. "But this material covers the whole planet!"

"I don't get it," said Coo. "How can a planet be made from eggshell?"

"Easy," said Arx. "Because Platus Two *isn't* a planet after all! It's an *egg*! A SPECIAL, GIGANTIC, PLANET-SIZED EGG!"

Everyone stared at him in amazement.

"Of course!" breathed Teggs. "It makes perfect sense!"

"Seems crazy to me," said Dippa.

"Ah, but things aren't always as they seem," said Teggs. "Remember the way the oviraptor ship was hidden inside the meteor? This is the same idea – only there's something a lot bigger hidden inside this planet!"

Arx turned to Professor Sog. "I *told* you Platus Two had grown!" he cried. "It's probably been getting bigger and bigger for hundreds of years – because the creature *inside it* has been growing in size too!"

"But – but eggs don't grow!" protested Sog.

"This is no ordinary egg," said Arx. "Besides, can *you* imagine laying an egg the size of a planet?"

"Ouch!" Teggs winced. "That would

bring tears to your eyes!"

"So let me get this straight," said Gipsy excitedly. "The explorers mistook Platus Two for a planet, just like we did. But deep inside it is the biggest baby in the universe — and it's starting to hatch!"

"That's why there are cracks all over the place!" said Teggs. "The thick shell is breaking open!"

"What about those geysers?" asked Coo. "How can an egg spray molten lava everywhere?"

"But it's *not* molten lava," Gipsy told him. "It's just egg white bursting out as the egg starts to hatch!"

"Well, what about that scary noise?" asked Dippa.

"Come on," said Arx, like a stern

schoolteacher. "What's the first thing a baby does when it hatches?"

"It cries!" Dippa realized. "That's what we've been hearing!"

They all stared down into the deep, dark hole, where the baby was slowly stirring in its runny yolk.

"Think how big it must be," whispered Sog. "Simply enormous! That movement we saw was probably just an eyelash! Or the tip of a whisker!"

"Uh-oh," said Gipsy. "I just had an awful thought. If this creature really *is* ready to hatch, then Platus Two must be close to completely cracking up!"

"I know how it feels," sighed Coo.

"Guys," said Teggs gravely, "if we can't get off this egg-world – we're doomed!"

"You're right!" Sog squealed. "We'll all be flung off into space!"

"Flung off into space?" said someone behind them. "Ha! That will seem like fun compared to what *I'm* going to do to you all!"

Teggs turned to find King Albu creeping along the ledge towards them, his red eyes agleam. The oviraptors had tracked them down!

"Quick!" Teggs shouted. "Run for it!"

But then Prince Goopo led his brothers out of the shadows, blocking their way.

King Albu giggled with glee. "This time, there will be no escape!"

Chapter Nine

A STICKY END

"Listen, you egg-mad maniac!" shouted
Teggs. "This whole world is about to
break apart! We have to get out of here
– and fast. If we work together, maybe
we can—"

"Nope." King Albu shook his head.

"I'm not doing a single thing until I've eaten those eggs. So *nyah!*"

Coo lumbered forwards. "All right then," he said. "I suppose you'd better have them."

"No!" shouted Dippa. "I won't let you!" She slammed her mighty tail down on the ground in front of Coo.

Coo froze. Everyone stared at Dippa in amazement — even King Albu.

"Captain Teggs is right," she said. "Those eggs are our future, Coo. And the future is worth fighting for."

"It is?" Coo blinked in surprise. "Oh. Well, if you really think so . . ."

Dippa smiled at Teggs. "I *know* so."

"You know nothing!" spat King Albu. "Come on! Eggs! Now!"

But even as he spoke, the ground started to shake. A fountain of steaming hot goo burst out from the deep dark hole in the ground.

"See that, King Albu?" Teggs yelled. "That's *egg white.* This whole place is bursting with the stuff! Why are you bothering with a few measly plateosaurus eggs?

The biggest, rarest egg in the whole universe is right under your feet!"

"Egg white?" King Albu started to drool. "Goopo, taste it at once."

Goopo edged forwards, keeping his gun aimed at Teggs. He dipped a long finger in the goop, then sucked it clean.

At once, a dreamy smile spread over his face. "It – it's the best egg I've ever tasted!" he shrieked.

Goopo threw away his gun and dived into the sticky stream. It whooshed him right up to the top of the fountain. He balanced there, guzzling the liquid as if it was lemonade.

"Get out of that!" yelled King Albu. "It's mine!"

He jumped into the fountain, which carried him high up into the air. He and Goopo bobbed about on the thick goo together, eating all they could.

"It's true!" shrieked the king. "It's the eggiest egg-juice I ever tasted! Come on, boys – tuck in!"

Prince Hibbit dived into the fountain and the others followed him, crying for joy. They were like mad birds flapping about in a giant's birdbath.

All except Prince Shelly. He stood and stared at his father and brothers in horror.

"Stop it!" he shouted. "You heard Captain Teggs – this whole place is about to break up! We must get out of here!"

But the oviraptors were far too busy filling their faces to listen. They didn't even notice when the fountain suddenly got smaller . . .

"Albu! Goopo! Look out!" Teggs yelled.

"Get out of there, you lot, quick!" added Shelly.

But it was too late.

As quickly as it had come, the egg–white fountain dried up to a dribble. As the thick liquid fell away, for a

moment King Albu and his boys were
left dangling in mid-air. Then, with a
loud yell, they fell — right down into
the deep hole.

"It must be miles down to the
bottom!" said Arx.

They heard a quiet, distant splash.
And then the scary wailing noise
started up again. "Put me down!" they

heard King Albu squawk in the distance. "I'll have you poached in butter for this!"

But then a terrible munching sound filled the air.

"The egg strikes back," said Teggs grimly.

"I tried to stop them," sighed Shelly.

"You did everything you could," Gipsy agreed.

"Come on," said Arx. "That thing is waking up, and it's hungry. We don't want to wind up as pudding!"

"You're right," said Teggs. "There's no time to lose."

"What about him?" Dippa scowled at Shelly. "If he comes with us he might eat our eggs!"

Shelly shook his head. "Believe me,
I've lost my appetite!"

"Enough talk," yelled Teggs. "Back to
the *Sauropod*! RUN!"

They ran for their lives.

The egg-planet rumbled and shook.
Geysers of egg white spurted up all
around them. The sky was darker than
ever, and it was hard to see anything
very clearly.

But somehow, they found their way back to the ship.

"Iggy!" yelled Teggs, panting for breath in the doorway. "Are you there?"

"Phew!" gasped Sog. "What's that terrible smell?"

"Must be Iggy and the boys," said Gipsy. "They've been working hard on our dung problem!"

Iggy appeared round the corner. He looked tired and red-faced, and his scaly hide was dripping with engine oil.

"We need to take off straight away," said Teggs. "Is that OK?"

Everyone stared at Iggy, hope burning in their eyes.

"Sorry, Captain," said Iggy, shaking his head. "We've got all the dung we need, but the engines are still stone-cold. And it'll take hours to burn enough dung for take-off!"

"But we don't *have* hours!" said Teggs.

Coo hung his head. The precious egg boxes fell to the floor. "Then . . . we can't escape!" he sighed. "It's all been for nothing!"

Chapter Ten

THE END OF THE EGG

"Wait a minute," said Dippa. "We can't take off, right?"

"Right," said Teggs.

She turned to Professor Sog. "And if we stay, we'll be flung off into space like you said, right?"

"It's true," he said sadly. "No one could survive such a thing."

"*We* certainly couldn't," Dippa agreed. "But maybe the *Sauropod* could — with us safely inside it!"

Arx hooted for joy. "She's right! There's still a chance! If this jumbo egg is going to hatch, we don't *need* to take off! The egg will launch us into space as it breaks up."

Teggs grinned at her. "Good thinking, Dippa." He turned to Iggy. "Do you think the *Sauropod* can stand it?"

Iggy shrugged. "She's a tough old ship . . . but I just don't know!"

"Well, I think we're about to find out," said Gipsy.

Just outside, a big split in the ground had opened up.

"Quick! Everyone to the flight deck!" yelled Teggs. "Find something to hold on to!"

Minutes later, the flight deck was filled to bursting with worried dinosaurs.

Iggy and his ankylosaurs had strapped themselves to the walls.

Gipsy, Teggs and Sog squashed up
together in the control pit. Arx sat at his
post, studying his instruments. Prince
Shelly sat nervously beside him. Dippa
and Coo huddled together, clinging to
their egg boxes. The alarm pterosaur
perched with the flight crew. She gave a
nervous squawk now and then.

Everyone had gathered together.
Perhaps for the last time.

Beneath the ship, the ground started to boil and buckle.

"Platus Two is cracking up," Arx reported.

"Hold tight, everybody," Teggs called. "And good luck."

They watched the egg-planet's last moments on the scanner screen.

The cracks in the ground grew wider and darker. They spat sticky goo high in the air. The *Sauropod* rattled and shook.

Then the distant horizon seemed to crack open. Something enormous burst out from beneath. It was groping around as if trying to grab the last stars in the sky.

"It's a claw!" cried Teggs. "A giant claw!"

More and more jagged cracks appeared in the shaking shell.

"This is it!" cried Arx. "Here we go!"

And suddenly, there was a terrific *crack!* as the egg-planet burst apart.

The scanner screen glowed white-hot. The *Sauropod* was sent spinning. No ship had ever stood up to such incredible force.

"You can do it," Teggs whispered. "I know you can!"

And at last, after what seemed like hours and hours . . . the shaking and the spinning stopped.

For a long time no one moved. No one even dared to speak.

It was left to Teggs to break the silence. "We made it!" he shouted. "We actually made it!"

The flight deck rang with the sound of happy cheers and squawking.

Cautiously, Professor Sog wriggled out from Teggs's armpit. "Look!" he gasped. "On the screen!"

The blackness of space was littered with pieces of broken shell. They gleamed like bits of china in the starlight.

Then something incredible burst into view. It looked like an enormous winged serpent. Its gleaming, golden body stretched out through the stars like

a comet's tail. Slowly, it opened its jaws and breathed out a big ball of fire as bright as the sun.

"Wait a minute," said Arx. "That looks like . . ."

"It can't be!" gasped Sog.

"It is!" cried Teggs. "It's a star dragon, it must be! The Jurassic Explorers searched the galaxy, but never found one."

Arx beamed. "And now we've seen one with our own eyes!"

"In honour of my greatest heroes," said Teggs, "I name this star dragon Jurassic."

Jurassic the star dragon performed a slow somersault. Then she flapped away into the endless night on four massive, golden wings.

"I'm glad Jurassic hatched safely," said Gipsy softly. "I wonder where she'll go now?"

"To warm herself by a sun, perhaps," suggested Sog. "Or maybe to find her friends in a far-off galaxy. Who knows?"

Iggy smiled. "I'm sure there's a home big enough for her somewhere."

"Maybe we'll see her again some day," said Teggs happily. "And find out for sure."

They watched Jurassic slowly disappear, off on her long journey through the stars. Then Iggy disappeared too, to check on his precious engines.

"What about us? What about our home?" sighed Coo. "Where can we go with our eggs?"

Dippa smiled. "Cheer up, Coo. Like the star dragon — we'll find somewhere."

Prince Shelly hopped over. "I am so sorry for all the trouble my family caused you. Will you let me try to make it up to you?"

"Good for you, Shelly," said Teggs. "You're a very unusual oviraptor!"

"That's for sure," Shelly smiled. "To tell you the truth . . . eggs bring me

out in a rash!"

Arx chuckled. "Hey! You're now King Albu's only son. That makes *you* the king!"

"You're right!" Shelly said thoughtfully. "You know, my family owns a holiday moon near Pluto Springs. I went there once, as a hatchling – it's sunny and grassy and very quiet."

Dippa stared at him. "So?"

"So, I guess it's mine now." He smiled at her and Coo. "And I'd love to give it to you two! You can live there for as long as you like."

"Will we be safe from other oviraptors?" asked Coo.

"I promise," said Shelly. "King Albu's mad menus are a thing of the past. From now on, we'll leave you in peace!"

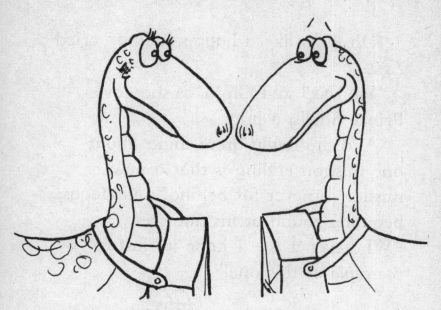

Dippa grinned at Coo. "Looks like we've got a new home out of this trip after all!"

Suddenly, the *Sauropod* lurched forwards. The sound of mighty engines firing filled the flight deck.

"Captain!" cried Iggy, jogging up to Teggs. "The heat of that explosion has warmed up the engines. We're ready to go back home!"

"First stop, Pluto Springs!" grinned Teggs.

"Oh, I do like a happy ending," cried Arx.

"Me too," said Gipsy, as she gave Prince Shelly a hug.

"And the really great thing about one mission ending is that a new mission is never far behind," said Teggs, beaming round at his fine crew. "Whatever it is — I hope it's just as *egg-citing* as this one!"

THE END

Turn over for
Astro Puzzle Time!

ASTRO PUZZLE TIME

THE HATCHING HORROR
WORDSEARCH

```
P R O F E S S O R B M J
N G Z D I E T P Y A X U
T O N U D Q E F R G B R
E O M T E G G S C I M A
S P J K C F O K X P E S
Z O F R A B S H G S U S
I R M P L S A J P Y L I
Y G S E B X U R I J Y C
B C G A U T R W X C G L
O G D Y L K V O U R N D
S Q O V I R A P T O R S
S P A C E S H I P A K H
```

IGGY
JURASSIC
STEGOSAUR
PROFESSOR
TEGGS
OVIRAPTORS
GOOPO
GIPSY
SPACESHIP
ALBU
EGGS
ARX

Reading across, up, down and diagonally, see if you can find all the listed words in the grid above...

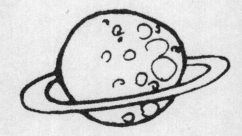

ASTRO PUZZLE TIME

THE HATCHING HORROR
QUIZ Questions:

1. Where were the Plateosaurus going to take their eggs?

2. What was the name of the Professor who was helping them?

3. Who first discovered Platus Two?

4. What did Gipsy wear on her wrist when she landed there?

5. What happens to Prince Shelly when he eats eggs?

Answers:

5. He comes out in a rash.

4. The special tracker.

3. The Jurassic Explorers.

2. 509.

1. Platus Two.

Read on for a sneak peek at the next
Astrosaurs adventure

The Seas of Doom!

Chapter One

A SOGGY MISSION

In orbit high above the planet Aqua
Minor, Captain Teggs Stegosaur was
waiting to start his next adventure.

He was waiting *very* impatiently.

"Admiral Rosso had
better call us soon," he
grumbled, chomping
on the delicious
ferns that covered his
control pit. "I can't
wait to find out why
we've been sent to the

sent to the soggiest planet in the Jurassic Quadrant!"

"I'm sure it won't be much longer, Captain," said Arx Orano, the triceratops beside him. He knew that sitting around twiddling his thumbs wasn't easy for his young, daredevil captain. Teggs didn't have any thumbs, for a start.

Teggs commanded the DSS *Sauropod*, the finest ship in the Dinosaur Space Service. He and his crew were all highly trained astrosaurs. They flew through space helping plant-eaters in peril – wherever the planet, whatever the risk.

But why had the *Sauropod* been sent to a world full of *fish*?

"Maybe Admiral Rosso thinks we need a holiday by the seaside," said Iggy Tooth, the *Sauropod*'s Chief Engineer.

"There *is* no seaside on Aqua Minor. Only sea!" said Gipsy Saurine, a duck-billed hadrosaur who handled the ship's communications and much more besides.

"Calling Captain Teggs . . ." the gruff voice of Admiral Rosso, the crusty barosaurus in charge of the Dinosaur Space Service, suddenly crackled from the *Sauropod*'s speakers. "Captain Teggs, can you hear me?"

"At last!" spluttered Teggs through a mouthful of moss. He rose up from the control pit.

Gipsy Saurine trotted over to Teggs. "Shall I put the admiral on the scanner screen, Captain?" she asked.

"Yes please," said Teggs.

Gipsy whistled the order through her snout to the dimorphodon. These plucky pterosaurs were the *Sauropod*'s flight crew, and they loved to be bossed about. The team leader flapped down and pecked the scanner control happily with his beak. A moment later, Admiral Rosso's wrinkled face appeared.

"Ah, there you are, Teggs," said the old barosaurus. "Sorry to keep you waiting, but running an entire space fleet keeps me busy. And when you get to my age . . ."

Teggs saluted. "What's up, sir?"

"It's what's *down* that's worrying us," said Admiral Rosso. "Down below!"

Arx and Gipsy swapped puzzled looks. But Teggs just smiled at the thought of a brand new adventure beginning at last.

"Something very big and very dangerous is swimming about in the seas of Aqua Minor," the admiral went on. "The cryptoclidus who go fishing there are getting very worried."

Teggs frowned. "Crypto-who?"

"A race of sea reptiles from the planet Cryptos," Arx explained. "They have run out of food on their own world, so now they fish the waters of Aqua Minor for squid and shellfish. Then they send it by rocket to the folks back home."

"Very good, Arx," smiled Admiral Rosso. "Teggs, you have a first-rate first officer there!"

"He's the best," Teggs agreed. "So, what's been happening on Aqua Minor?"

"Five undersea fish factories have been wrecked, along with several submarines." Admiral Rosso sighed. "But no one knows who's doing it — or why!"

Teggs nodded. "And you want us to find out."

Read the rest of
THE SEAS OF DOOM
to find out if Teggs can
solve the mystery!

Visit www.**stevecolebooks**.co.uk for fun, games, jokes, to meet the characters and much, much more!

Welcome to a world where dinosaurs fly spaceships and cows use a time-machine . . .

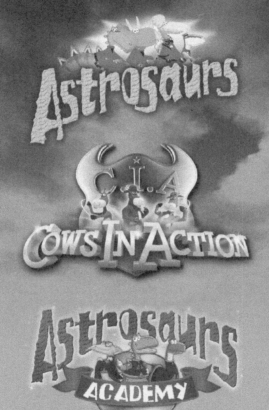

Sign up for the Steve Cole monthly newsletter to find out what your favourite author is up to!